Before reading

Look at the book cover to
Ask, "What do you think w

To build independence, th
at the start of this book. If the child needs extra practice, turn
back to pages 6 and 7 in 8a and read the words again with
the child.

During reading

Offer plenty of support and praise as the child reads the story.
Listen carefully and respond to events in the text.

When a **Key Word** is used for the first time, it is also shown at
the bottom of the page. If the child hesitates over a word, point
to the **New Key Words** box and practise reading it together.
If the word is phonically decodable, you can sound out the
letters and blend the sounds to read the word ("d-o-g, dog").
Praise the child for their effort, then return to the story.

Pause every few pages and ask questions to check the child's
understanding of what they have read. If they begin to lose
concentration, stop reading and save the page for later.

Celebrate the child's achievement and come back to the
story the next day.

After reading

After reading this book, ask, "Did you enjoy the story? What did
you like about it?" Encourage the child to share their opinions.

Use the comprehension questions on page 54 to check the
child's understanding and recall of the text.

Ladybird

Series Consultant: Professor David Waugh
With thanks to Kulwinder Maude

LADYBIRD BOOKS

UK | USA | Canada | Ireland | Australia
India | New Zealand | South Africa

Ladybird Books is part of the Penguin Random House group of companies whose addresses can be found at global.penguinrandomhouse.com.
www.penguin.co.uk   www.puffin.co.uk   www.ladybird.co.uk

Penguin Random House UK

Original edition of Key Words with Peter and Jane first published by Ladybird Books Ltd 1964
Series updated 2023
This book first published 2023
002

Text copyright © Ladybird Books Ltd, 1964, 2023
Illustrations by Flora Aranyi
Based on characters and design by Gustavo Mazali
Illustrations copyright © Ladybird Books Ltd, 2023

Printed in China

The authorized representative in the EEA is Penguin Random House Ireland, Morrison Chambers, 32 Nassau Street, Dublin D02 YH68

A CIP catalogue record for this book is available from the British Library

ISBN: 978-0-241-51095-7

All correspondence to:
Ladybird Books
Penguin Random House Children's
One Embassy Gardens, 8 Viaduct Gardens, London SW11 7BW

MIX
Paper from responsible sources
FSC® C018179

Key Words

with Peter and Jane

8b

So many things to do!

Based on the original
Key Words with Peter and Jane
reading scheme and research by William Murray

Original edition written by William Murray
This edition written by Shari Last
Illustrated by Flora Aranyi
Based on characters and design by Gustavo Mazali

"We have so many things to do today," said Mum.

Jane walked down the stairs.
"I have my swimming clothes," she said.

"And I have my football clothes," Peter said.

"Do you have your red football trainers, Peter?" Mum asked.

Peter grabbed his red football trainers, and they all walked out of the door.

New Key Words

many	today	clothes
football	your	door

7

"How many things are we doing today?" asked Jane.

"So many!" said Mum. "First, we are going to the swimming pool. Next is your football game. After that, you are going to Amber's party."

"Yes!" said Peter. "It's Amber's birthday party today. The party is in her garden."

New Key Words

| first | pool | next |
| party | birthday | garden |

9

The swimming pool was very big. Peter and Jane had their swimming classes with many other children.

Mum sat down next to the pool and looked at the children. Jane swam up and down the pool. She was a very quick swimmer. Peter splashed about in the pool.

"Mum!" Peter said. "I am having fun in the big pool!"

New Key Words

very   am

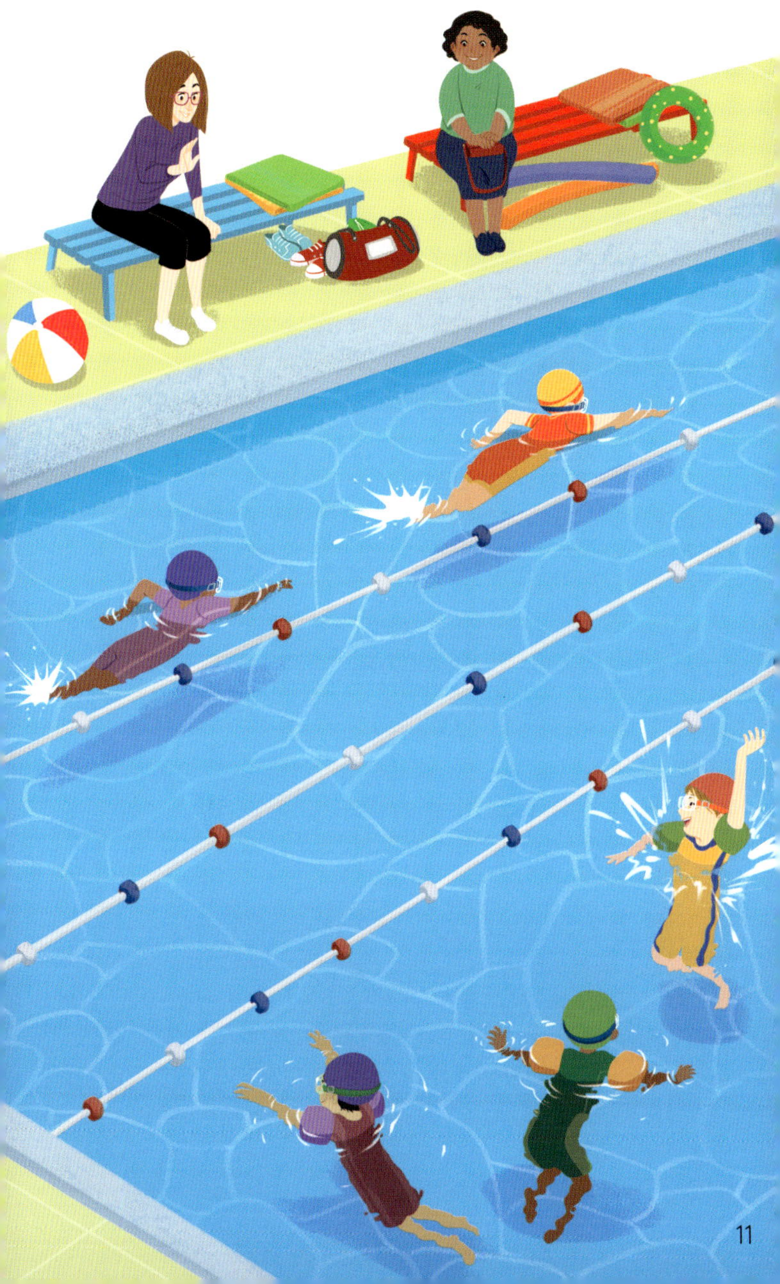

Next to the big pool was a round baby pool. There was a baby swimming with his mum in this pool.

Peter and Jane looked at the baby. He was playing with baby toys in the pool.

"There are no baby toys in the big pool," said Peter.

"That's because we're older now," said Jane. "You're not a baby."

New Key Words

round   baby   because   old

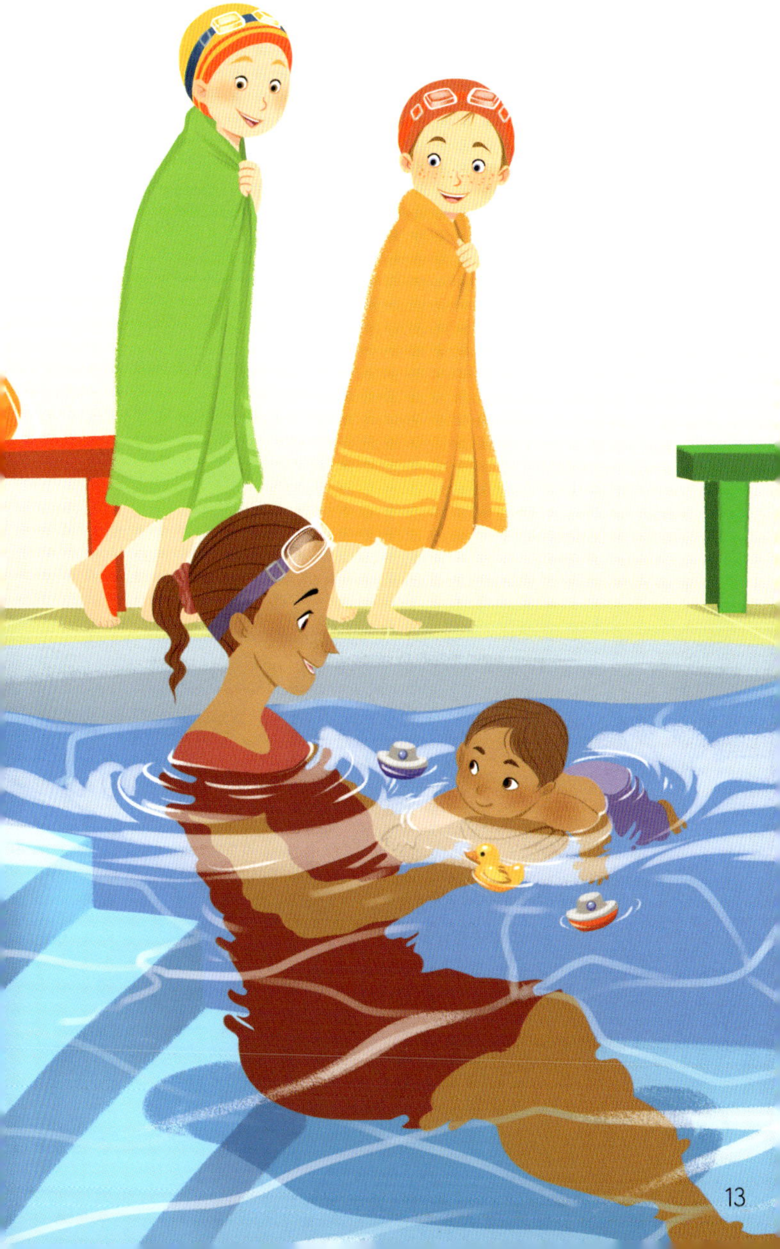

After swimming in the pool, the children put on their red football clothes because it was time for a football match at the park.

Peter and Jane lived near the park, so Dad met them at the football pitches.

"I am on time for the match today!" he said. Dad had Tess with him.

Jane played football on the green pitch, and Peter played football on the red pitch.

New Key Words

time   live

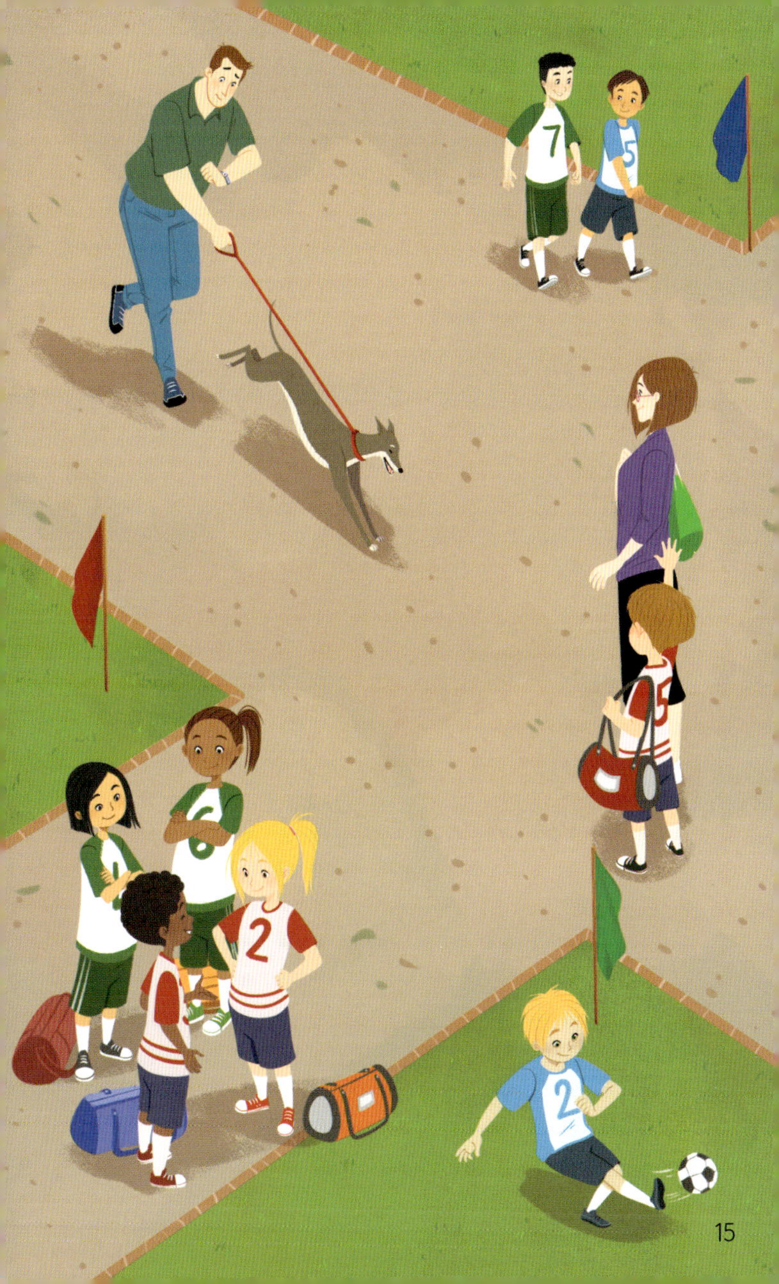

Jane kicked the football round a player from the other team and . . . GOAL!

"You are really good, Jane!" said Dad. "This is your best football match yet."

"It's because we play football in the garden every day," Jane said.

New Key Words

every   day

17

Peter was running round the red football pitch. He kicked the ball away from many of the children on the other team.

Peter had not kicked the ball in the goal before. But today, when he saw the goal, he kicked the football very hard and . . . GOAL!

"Go, Peter!" yelled Mum.

New Key Words

      away   before   when

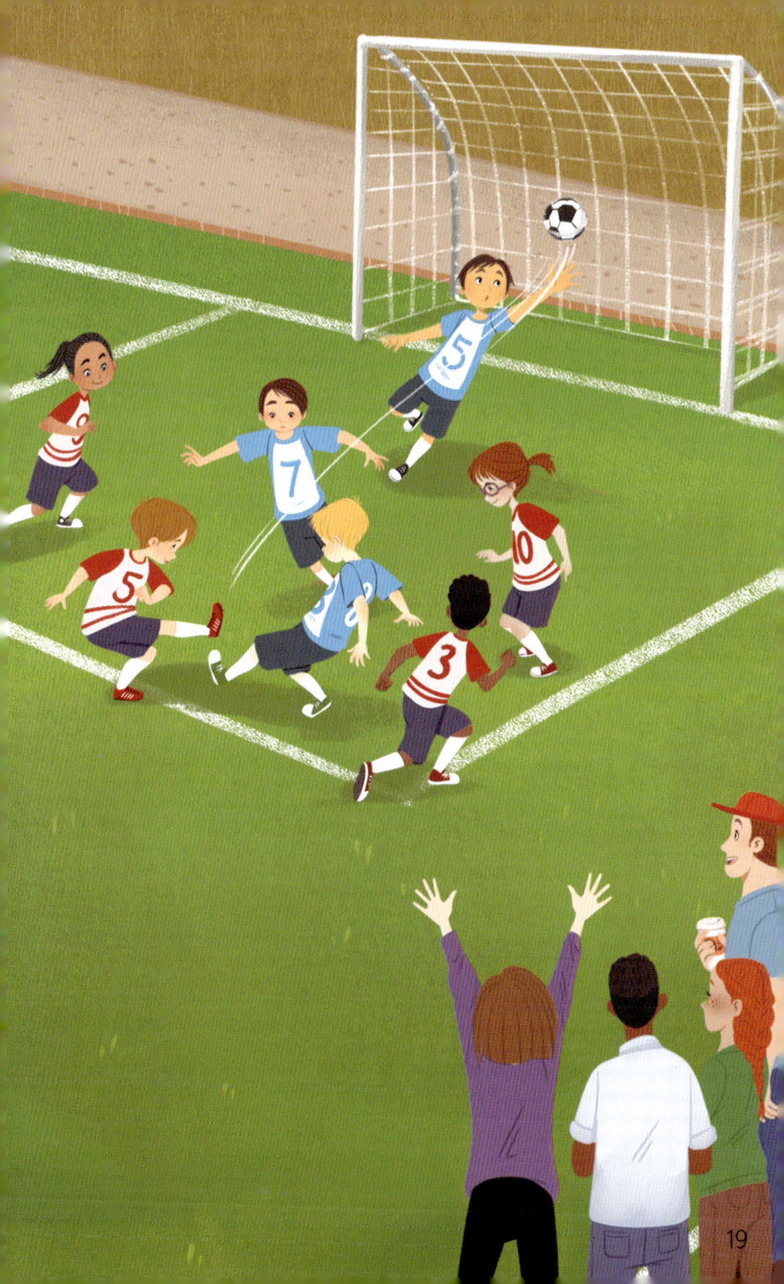

After the football match, Jane asked, "Can we eat now?"

"Yes, can we?" asked Peter.

"We have a surprise for you," said Dad. "We are going to have lunch in a cafe, because of your good goals in your football matches today!"

"Thanks!" said the children.

"Are we going to the one next door to the clothes shop?" asked Peter.

"We are," said Mum.

New Key Words

surprise

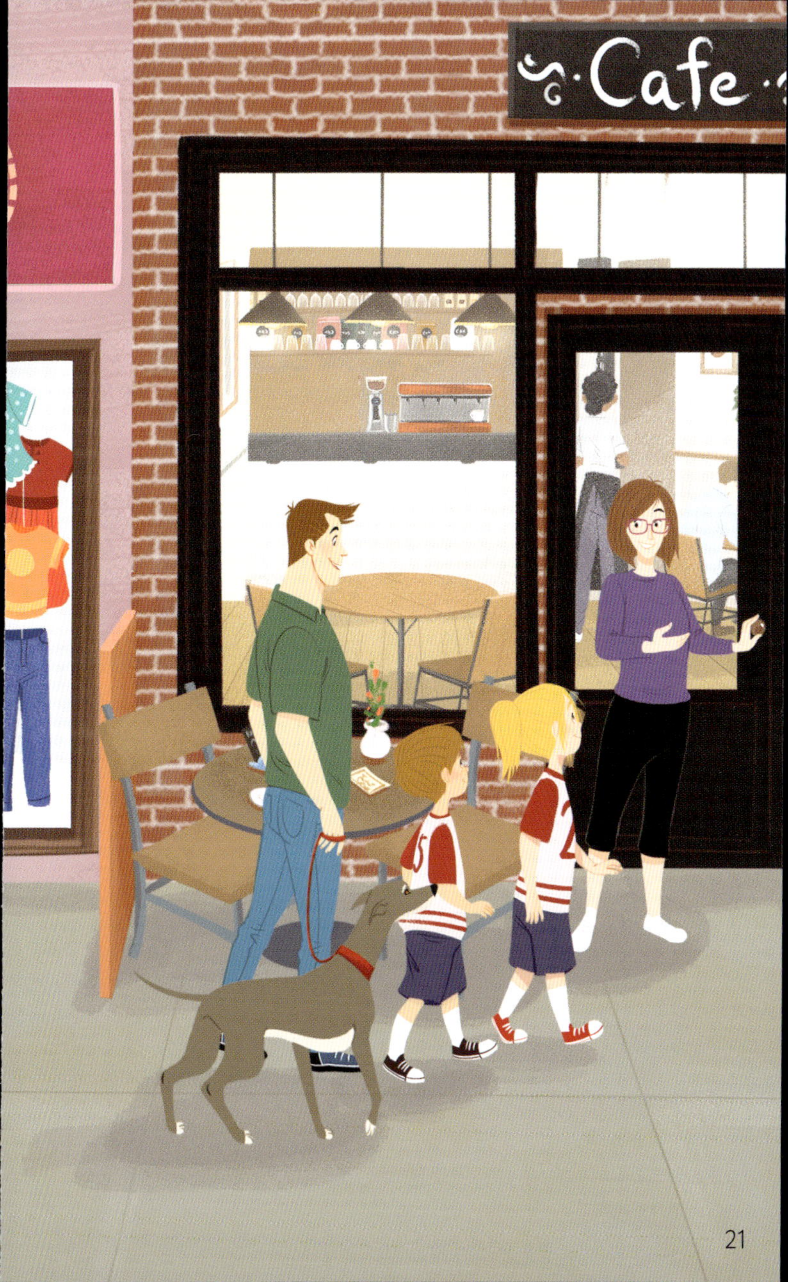
Cafe

The cafe had three free chairs near the door.

"I will find one more chair," said Dad.

When Dad pulled up a chair, they all sat down and picked their meals. First, Peter and Jane had fish and chips to eat. Next, they had fruit.

"This has been the best surprise," said Jane.

"Yes," said Peter. "I like surprises!"

New Key Words

three   find   been

23

"We have Amber's birthday party next," said Dad.

"Amber's party is starting soon!" said Peter. "We must get home now."

"You must find fresh clothes and clean up," said Mum. "You can't go to the party in your football clothes."

New Key Words

25

At home, Peter said, "I'll find the birthday gifts for Amber."

"I'll draw her a birthday picture," said Jane. "I will draw a big six."

The picture said, "You are six years old today."

"I am six years old now, like Amber," said Peter. "I will be one year older on my next birthday."

New Key Words

        draw   year

27

"I want to be on time for Amber's party," said Peter.

"We will be. Amber lives next door, Peter!" said Mum.

"Is it a surprise party like Granny's was?" Jane asked Mum.

"No," said Mum, "it's not a surprise party today."

New Key Words

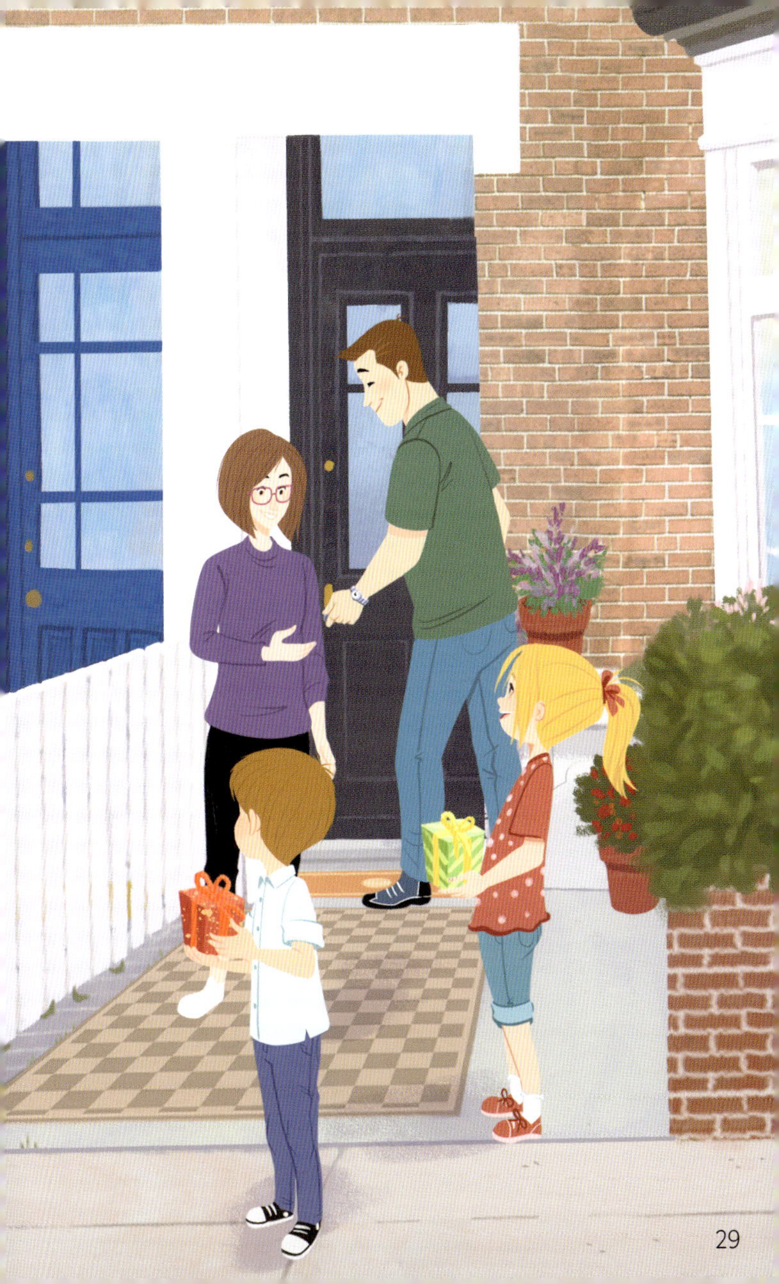

Peter and Jane walked round to Will, Amber and Maya's house.

They had been to many birthday parties there before.

When they saw Amber at the door, Peter and Jane yelled, "It's your birthday!"

New Key Words

31

The birthday party was set up in Amber's garden. Peter and Jane looked at the many things to eat.

"First, here is your birthday gift from me, Amber," said Peter.

"And next, here is your birthday gift from me!" said Jane.

Maya looked at Jane's birthday picture for Amber. "I like it!" said Maya.

New Key Words

33

Amber's birthday party was fun. The children played party games and worked on birthday pictures.

"When is it time for the birthday buns, Mum?" asked Maya.

"First, we must sing a birthday song," said Maya's mum, Cass.

New Key Words

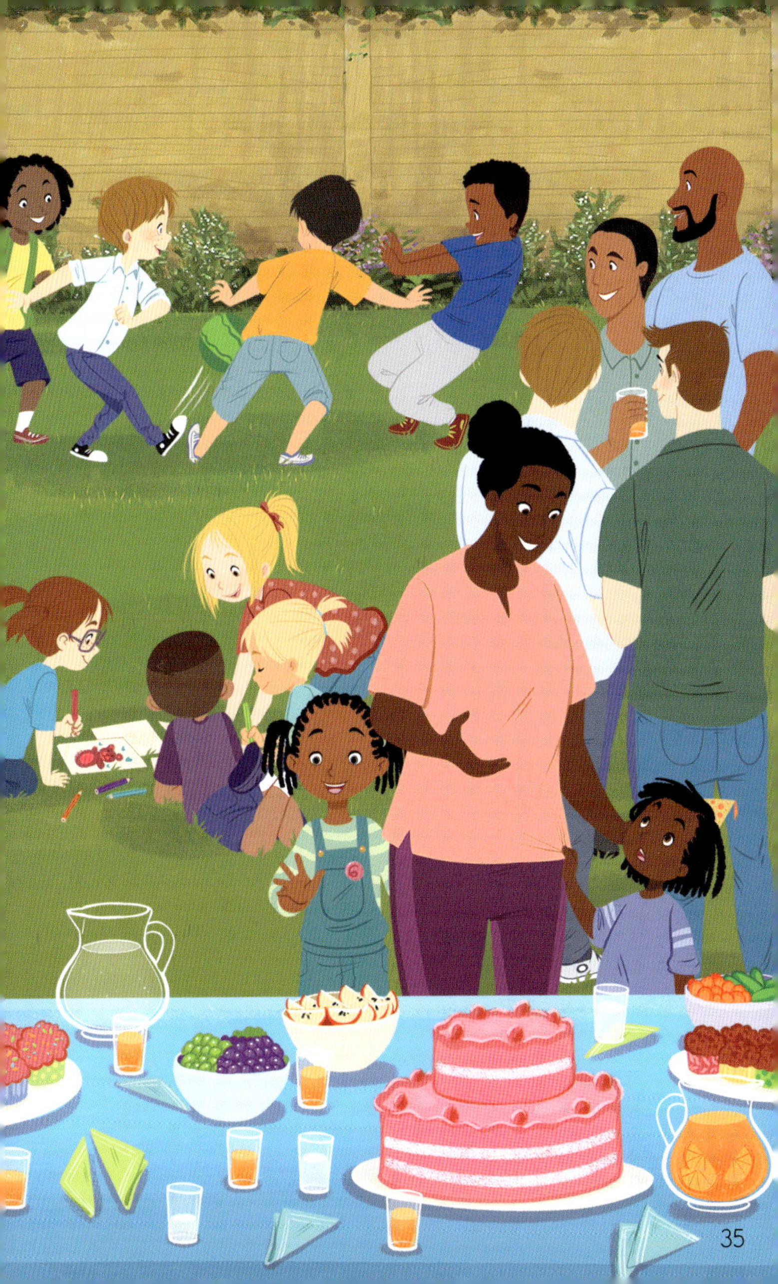

After playing party games, the children had something to eat. The older children helped the little children.

"Will gave me a bun first because it's my birthday," Amber said to Peter.

"Jane gave Maya a bun next because she is little," said Peter. "She is three years old. We are three years older than her now."

They all sat in the garden eating birthday buns.

New Key Words

gave

37

Next, Peter and Amber played with the rabbits.

"Rabbits don't like birthday buns," Amber said.

"But birds do," said Peter. "That baby bird is finding little bits of bun to eat."

The baby bird hopped round next to them. But, before long, Amber's cat surprised the bird!

New Key Words

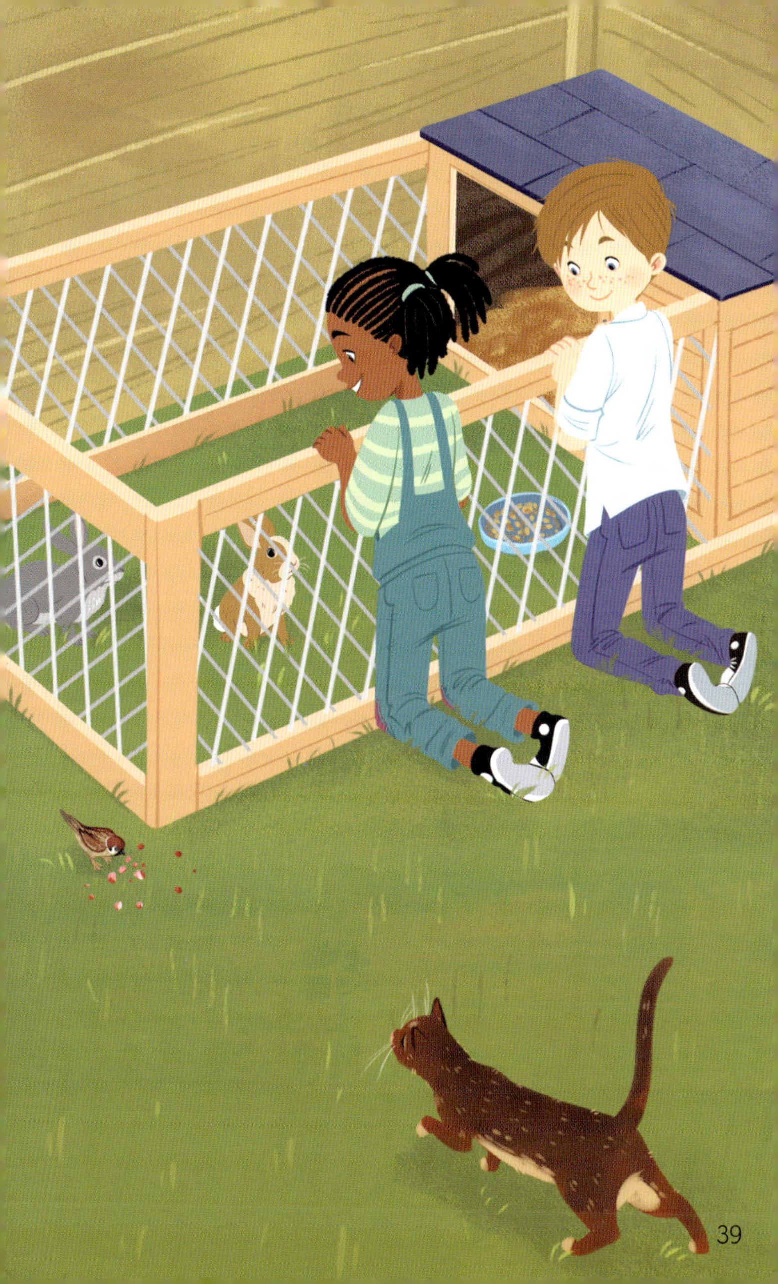

The garden was getting very hot because of the sun.

"You can splash your feet in the pool, if you like," said Cass.

"The pool! The pool!" said the children.

Amber's dad, Tim, said, "Put your feet in, but don't get your clothes wet!"

New Key Words

if

41

When it was time to go home, Cass and Tim gave every child a surprise gift.

"If you put your hand in the bag, you can find your surprise gift," said Tim.

Peter pulled out a book about football. Jane pulled out a set of three pens for drawing.

"Thank you, Amber," said Peter. "This was a fun party."

New Key Words

43

Before Peter and Jane hopped into bed, they worked on pictures of their day.

Jane's drawing was of the swimming pool. There was a round baby pool next to the big pool.

"The baby pool has toys in the water," said Jane.

New Key Words

45

Peter's drawing was of the birthday party.

"I can see the round birthday buns!" Jane said. "They look good!"

"I like your drawing of the baby bird," said Mum.

"On my next birthday, can I have a surprise birthday party in our garden?" asked Peter.

"It's not a surprise party if you ask for it, Peter!" said Dad.

New Key Words

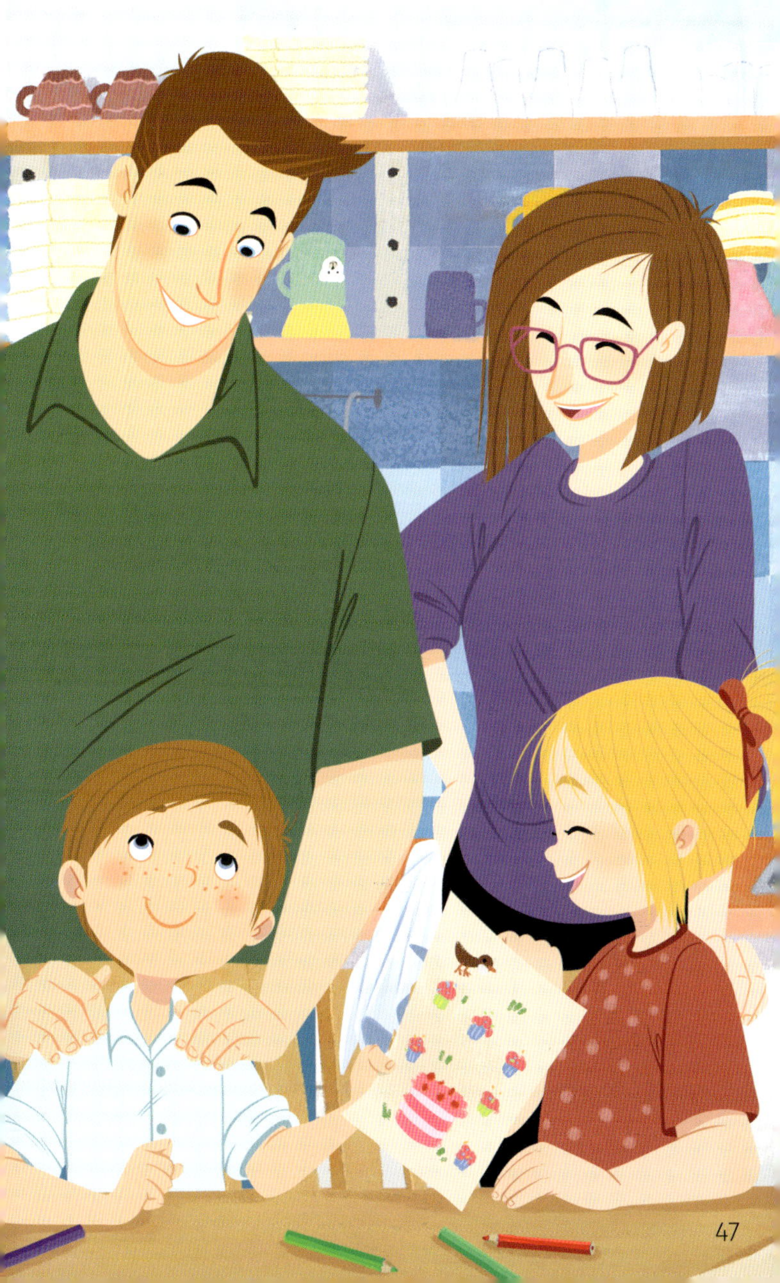

Now, Dad was drawing a picture.

"It's a drawing of you playing football today," he said. "That was the best football you've played all year! You surprised me with how good you are."

"I can't wait to play football in the garden again, Dad," said Jane.

New Key Words

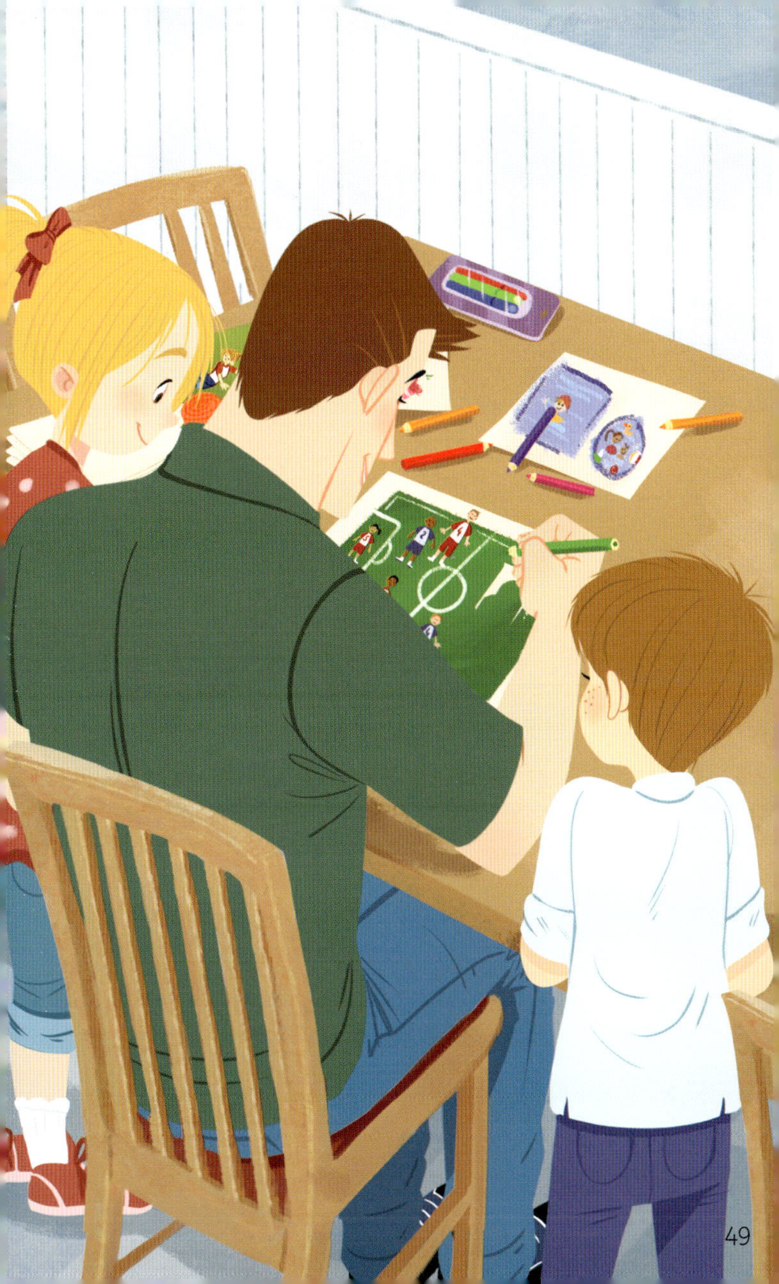

Mum had one more surprise for Peter and Jane before the end of the day.

"Because you are both so good at football now," she said, "we are going to let you stay up to see a big football match before bed."

"Wow, Mum!" yelled Peter.

"Thank you!" said Jane.

New Key Words

51

The children put on their clothes for bed and sat down next to Mum and Dad for the big football match.

They saw the football players run round the pitch many times.

"GOAL!" yelled Jane. She and her brother jumped up and down.

Today had been a good day for Peter and Jane.

New Key Words